Lee Aucoin, *Creative Director*
Jamey Acosta, *Senior Editor*
Heidi Fiedler, *Editor*
Produced and designed by
Denise Ryan & Associates
Illustration © Christine Jenny
Rachelle Cracchiolo, *Publisher*

Teacher Created Materials
5301 Oceanus Drive
Huntington Beach, CA 92649-1030
http://www.tcmpub.com
Paperback: ISBN: 978-1-4333-5572-1
Library Binding: ISBN: 978-1-4807-1717-6
© 2014 Teacher Created Materials

The Hare and the Tortoise

An Aesop Fable
Retold by Sarah Keane

Retold by Sarah Keane

Illustrated by Christine Jenny

Once upon a time, there was a hare who always boasted about how fast he could run. He laughed at the tortoise for carrying his house on his back. And he laughed at him for being so slow.

One day, the tortoise grew annoyed, so he argued
with the hare. "Who do you think you are? I know you
are very fast, but even you can be beaten!"

3

The hare just laughed. "Beaten in a race? Who could beat me in a race? Not you! I'm sure there's nobody in the world who could win against me. I'm so fast. Why don't you try?"

The tortoise accepted the challenge. He really
was annoyed. A course was planned. Early the next
morning, the hare and the tortoise stood at the
starting line.

The hare yawned as the tortoise plodded off slowly. When the hare saw how slow his rival was, he decided to take a quick nap. "Take your time!" he called to the tortoise. "I'll just have forty winks. I'll catch up with you in a minute."

After a while, the hare woke with a start. He gazed
around, looking for the tortoise. But the tortoise was
only a short distance away. He had not even managed
to cover half the course!

8

The hare breathed a sigh of relief. He decided he might as well have breakfast. So off he went to munch some lettuce in a nearby field.

But his big breakfast and the hot sun made the hare feel very tired. He glanced at the tortoise. He was now halfway along the course. The hare decided he would have another nap before he flashed past the finish line.

The hare smiled at the thought of racing by the tortoise. Then, he fell fast asleep.

The sun started to sink in the west. The tortoise, who had been plodding toward the finish line since morning, was very, very near it.

FINISH

FINISH

13

The hare woke with a start. He looked around and could barely see the tortoise in the distance. He leapt up and dashed away as fast as he could, gasping for breath as he ran. As he ran he thought, *I just have to run a little faster and I'll finish first.*

14

But the hare's last leap was too late. The tortoise had beaten him to the finish line. The hare felt tired and disgraced. He slumped down beside the tortoise.

"You know, slow and steady wins the race every time," the tortoise said to the hare.

The Hare's Story

As Told by the Hare

You should not believe Mr. Aesop's story! A member of the tortoise's family told it to him. Hares like me know the real story.

19

One day I said to the tortoise, "Oh, you are so slow. No wonder all the food is gone by the time you get there." He was very annoyed with me. I laughed when he said, "Who do you think you are? I know you are very fast, but even you can be beaten!"

"I'm sure there's nobody in the world who could win against me. I'm so fast. Why don't you try?" I cried. I must admit I was surprised when he accepted the challenge!

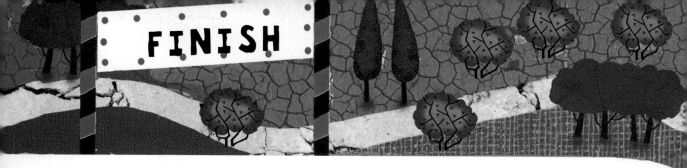

I'm sure the Tortoise Race Committee planned the course. There were far too many tight corners, rough sections, muddy patches, and thorny bushes. How was I supposed to run as fast as a speeding bullet when the track wasn't perfect? I'm used to being treated as a star from the Hares' Track and Field Team!

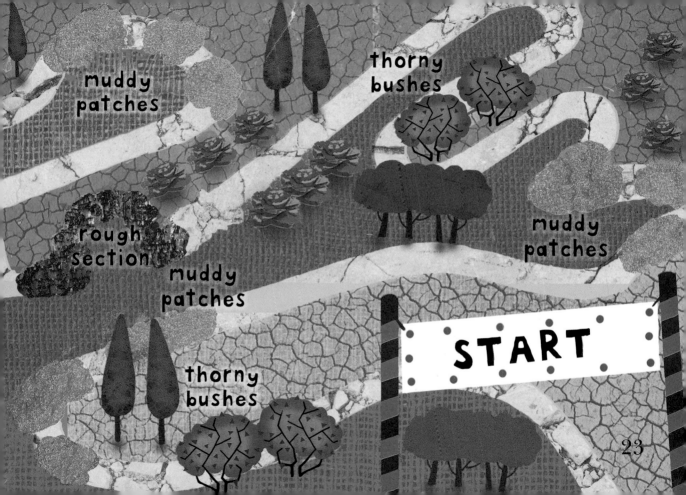

Mr. Aesop failed to tell you I did not hear the starting pistol. I was busy waving to all my fans. I did not realize the gun had gone off and the tortoise had already started the race! The tortoise certainly plodded off slowly, but you should know I started after him.

25

When I saw the tortoise moving so slowly, I did not decide to have a nap. I decided to stop and wrap my feet with leaves. Then, I would be able to run more easily over the muddy patches and around the thorny bushes. And of course, I realized I needed breakfast. So I went into the lettuce field and ate some juicy greens.

I didn't know a big breakfast and the hot day would make me sleepy. Not that it mattered. I knew I had plenty of time to have a long nap.

I was most surprised when I woke and saw the tortoise near the finish line. I'm sure the Tortoise Race Committee moved the line so the tortoise would get there first. And that's what *really* happened.

28